BESITOS DE LEJITOS, KISSES FROM A DISTANCE

WRITTEN BY NOEMI MENDEZ
Illustrated By Olivia Allard

Archway Publishing books may be ordered through booksellers or by contacting:

Archway Publishing
1663 Liberty Drive
Bloomington, IN 47403
www.archwaypublishing.com
844-669-3957

Interior Image Credit: Olivia Allard

ISBN: 978-1-6657-3596-4 (sc)
ISBN: 978-1-6657-3597-1 (e)

Print information available on the last page.

Archway Publishing rev. date: 1/9/2023

School will begin soon, and mami tells me to be very careful! "Pero ten mucho cuidado and try to keep your hands to yourself" said mami.

La escuela comenzará pronto, y mami me dice que tenga mucho cuidado. Pero ten mucho cuidado y trata de mantener tus manos para ti mismo" dijo mami.

"Remember to keep your distance! 6 feet apart is the rule to keep safe" said mami.

"¡Recuerda mantener tu distancia! A 6 pies de distancia es la regla para mantenerse a salvo" dijo mami.

"Be careful and keep your mask on if you need to" said mami.

"Ten cuidado y mantén tu máscara puesta si es necesario" dijo mami.

5

"Wash your hands and keep them sanitized"
said mami.

"Lávese las manos y manténgalas
desinfectadas" dijo mami.

Can I give my friends a hug?

"Only air hugs for now mija, de lejitos" said mami.

¿Puedo dar un abrazo a mis amigos?

"Solo abrazos aéreos por ahora mija, de lejitos" dijo mami.

What about my teacher, can I give her a hug?

"Only air hugs for now mija, de lejitos" said mami.

¿Qué pasa con mi maestra, puedo darle un abrazo?

"Solo abrazos aéreos por ahora mija, de lejitos" dijo mami.

What about kisses? Can I give my friends kisses on the cheek?

"Solamente besitos de lejitos!" said mami.

¿Qué pasa con los besos? ¿Puedo dar besos en la mejilla a mis amigos?

"Solamente besitos de lejitos!" dijo mami.

14

Solamente besitos de lejitos!

Just kisses from a distance!

Can I give
you a hug and
kisses?

¿Puedo darte
un abrazo y
besos a ti?

18

Si mija! Besitos y un fuerte abracito, because I will miss you all day long!

Yes mami! Kisses and one strong hug.

Si mija! Besitos y un fuerte abracito, ¡porque te extrañaré todo el día!

¡Sí mami! Besos y un fuerte abrazo.

I love you, mami! I love you too mijita!

¡Te amo, mami! ¡Te amo demasiado mijita!

Fin

The End

This book is dedicated to all those who lost loved ones during the pandemic. This book is also dedicated to all those parents who took their children to school in such unprecedented times but understood the importance of having their student at school.

I would also like to thank everyone who has supported me though this work. Thank you to my supportive husband Ronnie my children, Angie, Everett and Charisma and to all of my close friends who have always believed in me. Your kind words and encouragement keep me motivated to write the next book.

Words in Spanish translated to English

Besitos-kisses

De-from

Lejitos-distance

Mami-mom

Pero-but

Ten-be

Mucho-very

Cuidado-careful

Mija-daughter

Solamente-just

Si-yes

Fuerte-strong

Abracito-hug

Mijita-daughter

Editor Alba Perez

Alba is a consultant with an expansive career on diversity and inclusion in corporate Des Moines, Human Rights in Iowa and helping financial organizations reach and serve Latinos around the country. She was born, raised and educated in Honduras and studied at the University Nacional Autonoma de Honduras.

Illustrator Olivia Allard

Olivia is an artist, writer and student finishing her studies at the University of Iowa. As a child, her favorite stories had characters who looked like her and had lives that paralleled her own. So, as she moves on in her future, she hopes to tell her own diverse stories and connect with others through all art forms.

CPSIA information can be obtained
at www.ICGtesting.com
Printed in the USA
BVHW010216300123
657431BV00017B/665